Football things to make and do

Rebecca Gilpin

Designed and illustrated by
Josephine Thompson

Additional design and illustrations by
Vicky Arrowsmith,
Erica Harrison, Jessica Johnson,
Katie Lovell, Non Figg and
Samantha Meredith

Steps illustrated by
Jo Moore

Photographs by
Howard Allman

Contents

Corner kick drawing

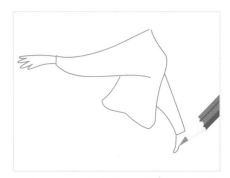

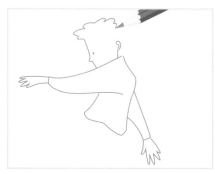

Draw studs on his kicking boot.

1. Pressing lightly with a pencil, draw a shape for a player's outstretched arm. Draw his body and his other arm, then draw both of his hands.

2. Draw a side-on face with a nose halfway down. Add an ear and a line for the back of the neck. Then, draw a dot for an eye and add some hair.

3. Draw the player's shorts, then add his legs, with one of them raised as if kicking a ball. Draw boots and socks, then add a ball up in the air.

You could draw two players, with one of them tackling to win the ball.

4. Draw a corner flag behind the player. Draw lines for the corner of the pitch, starting at the bottom of the flag. Add a curve across the corner, too.

Draw all the lines in the same direction.

5. Outline the player and flag with a sharp black pencil. Then, using a coloured pencil, fill in the face with lots of short diagonal lines.

The long lines will make it look as if the player is moving.

6. Fill in the hair. Then, draw lots of long lines down from the top arm, overlapping the black line. Fill in the shirt and other arm as well.

Add some movement lines around the ball, too.

7. Fill in the rest of the player and the flag. Outline the lines on the pitch with a sharp green pencil. Then, add grass and 'whoosh' lines up to the ball.

Footballer finger puppet

1. Cut a rectangle of thin white cardboard about the length of your hand. Draw a footballer's head near the top. Then, add a neck and a shirt below it.

You will use the shorts in step 4.

2. Draw a pair of shorts on a piece of bright paper and cut them out. Lay the shorts below the shirt and draw around them, then lift them off.

3. Draw the footballer's arms. Then, draw a circle for a finger hole on each leg. Fill in the footballer with felt-tip pens, then draw over the outlines.

Leave a thin white border around the footballer.

4. Cut around the footballer. Then, cut up to the circles and cut them out. Spread glue along the top of the shorts and press them on.

The back edge needs to be straight.

5. To make the boots and socks, draw a tall boot shape on thick paper. Make the top as wide as two fingers, like this. Then, cut out the shape.

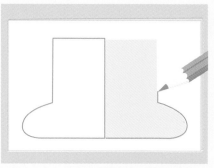

6. Fold a piece of white paper in half and lay the boot shape on it. Draw around the shape, then turn it over and draw around it again, like this.

Squeeze and roll a piece of foil into a ball, then flick your finger to 'kick' it.

4

Push your fingers through the holes, then push on the socks and boots. Your knuckles will be the footballer's knees.

The tab is used when you glue them together.

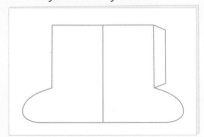

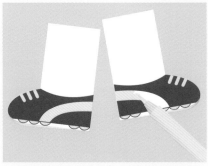

7. Draw a tab on one side of the boot shape, like this. Then, holding the layers together, cut around everything, including the tab, to make two boots.

8. Fold both of the boot shapes in half. Fold the tabs inside and spread glue on them. Then, press the shapes together to secure the edges.

9. Draw a curved line for the top of each boot, then add studs on the bottom. Decorate both sides of the boots with felt-tip pens.

Fan collage

Don't spread the glue right to the edges of the head.

1. Rip a shape for a body from paper from an old magazine, then glue it onto a piece of paper. Rip a circle for a head, then glue it onto the body.

Tuck the ears under the head a little.

2. Cut a rounded shape for a hat, then rip across its bottom edge. Glue the hat onto the head, then cut out two ears and glue them below the hat.

To make a cheering crowd like this, start with the fans at the top.

3. Rip a bobble for the hat and glue it on. Then, cut two curved arms and glue them onto the body. Rip two ovals for hands and glue them on, too.

Add lots of streamers by drawing curls with chalks or pencils.

4. Rip sleeves from magazine paper and glue them on. Draw eyes and a mouth on paper, then cut them out and glue them on. Draw a nose, too.

5. Cut two strips of paper and glue them together to make a flag. Glue on the flag and draw a handle, then glue a shape onto the shirt for a logo.

A fan with a scarf

For a scarf, cut two paper strips, then make lots of cuts in one end of each strip. Rip paper shapes for stripes, then glue them on.

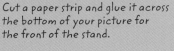

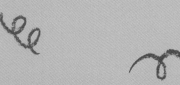

Cut a paper strip and glue it across the bottom of your picture for the front of the stand.

Simple footballer drawing

Make one leg look as if it is stretching out, like this.

Draw blobs for the hands — you will add fingers in step 6.

1. Use a bright chalk or chalk pastel to draw a footballer's shirt on a piece of green paper. Then, add a curved neckline with a white chalk.

2. Draw shorts with the white chalk, then add stripes with the bright chalk. Leave a gap for legs below the shorts, then draw shapes for socks.

3. Using a pale or darker brown chalk, draw a circle for the footballer's head, and add a neck below it. Then, draw the arms, hands and legs.

You could draw lots of footballers in different positions. Look at the sports pages of newspapers for ideas.

4. Draw the hair, then draw white ovals for football boots. Using black and white chalks, draw a football a little way above one foot.

5. Draw around the shirt with a thin black pen, then add a circle as a logo. Draw around the head, hair and neck, then draw a face, too.

6. Outline the arms, shorts, legs, socks and boots. Draw around the ball, then draw two movement lines below the ball with the white chalk.

You could draw two players heading the ball to each other.

You could draw a player dribbling a ball in and out of a line of markers.

Overhead kick door sign

Hook this part of the door sign over a door handle.

TOM'S ROOM

1. Draw around a large roll of sticky tape near the top of a piece of thick paper. Draw two lines down to the bottom of the paper, then cut out the shape.

Don't worry if the strips go over the edges.

2. Turn the shape over. Rip strips from wrapping paper or paper from old magazines. Glue them across the shape, then let the glue dry.

Use the lid of a spice jar if you have one.

3. Turn the paper shape over again and trim around the edges. Then, lay the lid from a small jar in the middle of the circle and draw around it.

4. To make the paper shape into a door sign, draw two curving lines (shown here in red). Then, cut along the lines and around the small circle.

Shirt — — Shorts

5. Turn the door sign over. Then, draw a shirt and a pair of shorts on scraps of paper. Cut them out and glue them onto the door sign, like this.

You could make a sign that you can press onto your door with poster tack instead.

6. Draw a head and neck on another piece of paper. Cut out the shape, then glue it on so that it overlaps the neck and the edge of the doorsign.

7. Draw an arm and two legs on some paper. Cut them out and glue them on. Cut out shapes for socks and boots and glue them on, too.

Glue the boots on before the socks.

8. Cut out a ball and glue it on. Glue on thin strips of paper beside it as movement lines. Then, write your name on the sign with a black pen.

You could draw stripes or other details on the shirt, too.

Zigzag match card

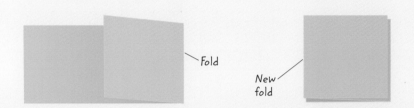

Fold

New fold

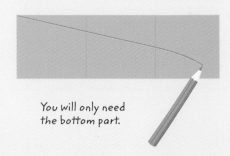

You will only need the bottom part.

1. Cut a long rectangle from green cardboard for the card. Fold one edge over until it is halfway along, like this, then press down the fold.

2. Turn the rectangle over and fold the other edge until it meets the first fold. Press down the new fold, then open out the card.

3. Draw a diagonal line across the card, making the right-hand end curve down a little, like this. Cut along the line, then fold the bottom part into a card.

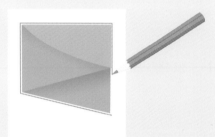

4. Turn the folded card upside down and lay it on a piece of thin white cardboard. Draw around the card with a pencil, then cut out the shape.

5. Using a thin black pen, draw the front of the stand across the bottom of the shape. Draw lots of fans in the crowd, then fill them in with pencils.

To make a card of a goal celebration, glue a goal onto the back part.

Make sure that some of the stand shows above the green paper.

6. Cut out the fans, leaving a white border around them. Spread glue along the bottom of the stand, then press it onto the back part of the card.

Fill in the two players with different pencils.

7. Draw a running player, a football and a defender on white cardboard. Fill them all in with pencils, then cut them out and turn them over.

8. Glue the bottom half of the defender onto the middle part of the card. Then, glue the running player and the football onto the front part.

Write your message below the fans on the back part of the card.

Flicking football game

1. For a player's base, hold one end of a pipe cleaner. Bend it a little way up, then wind the long part around and around the bend. Then, tuck in the end.

Put the base on a piece of old newspaper.

2. Draw around the base on thin cardboard. Cut out the circle, then dab a big blob of white glue onto it. Lay the base on top and press it down well.

You could make a pitch from a big sheet of green paper and paint or draw on white lines.

The weight of the coin helps the player to stand up.

3. Make more bases so that you have two teams with the same number of players in each team. When the glue is dry, tape a coin onto each base.

Use a different colour for each team.

4. Cut a shirt and pair of shorts for each player. Then, glue the shorts onto the shirts and decorate them all with felt-tip pens, like this.

Make the ball as round as you can, so that it rolls.

5. Tape the bases onto the back of the shirts to make the players. Then, cut out a square of foil, and squeeze it and roll it in your hands to make a ball.

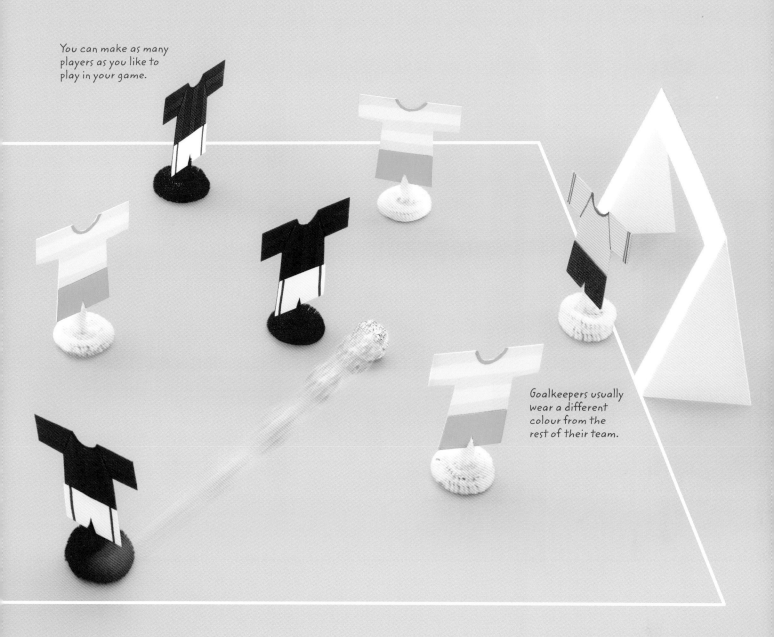

You can make as many players as you like to play in your game.

Goalkeepers usually wear a different colour from the rest of their team.

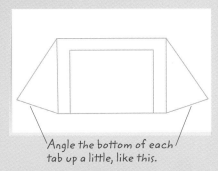

Angle the bottom of each tab up a little, like this.

6. Fold a piece of thin cardboard in half for the goals. Draw a rectangle, then draw a goal inside it. Then, add triangles on the sides for tabs.

7. Holding the layers together, cut around the whole shape. Then, cut out the goals. Fold back the tabs to make the sides of the goals, and stand them up.

How to play

You can play this on your own or with a friend. Position the players between the goals. Drop the ball into the middle, then the player who is closest to it takes the first 'kick'. To kick the ball, flick the player's base to make it hit the ball. The nearest player to the ball takes the next kick and so on.
If two players are equally close to the ball or a goal is scored, pick up the ball, drop it into the middle again and continue playing.

Football flickbook

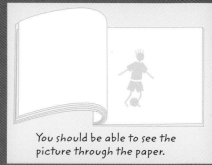

Make the squares 7 x 7cm.

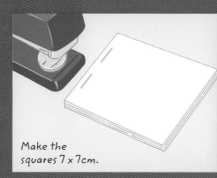

You should be able to see the picture through the paper.

1. Cut 14 squares from paper that is thin enough to see through for tracing. Pile up the squares neatly and staple them at one end.

2. Using a black pen, draw a footballer on the back page of the flickbook. Then, turn over the page in front, so that it covers your drawing.

Change the position of the football, too.

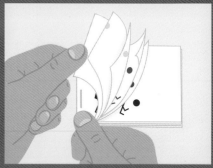

3. Draw over the picture, but change the position of the arms, body and legs a little. Draw pictures on the other pages, changing them each time.

4. Hold the flickbook in your hands and quickly flick through it from the back to the front. This makes it look as if the footballer is moving.

Pages from this flickbook are shown spread out so that you can see some of the different pictures.

The picture on the front page is the last one you see when you flick through the flickbook.

Draw a simple figure, as it's easier to keep it looking the same on all the pages.

Defensive wall paperchain

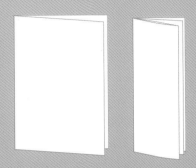

1. Fold a long rectangle of paper in half, with its short ends together. Then, fold the paper in half again and crease the folds well.

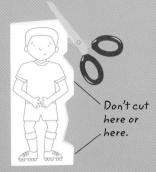

Don't cut here or here.

2. Draw a footballer with his elbows and feet near to the folds. Cut him out, but don't cut along the folds near the elbows and feet.

Make each player look different.

3. Unfold the paper to make a chain of four footballers standing in a defensive wall. Then, draw the other players and fill them in with pens.

League table

1

scarlet city

2

blue sky fc

3

forest athletic

4

union city

5

stripes united

6

ocean fc

7

bigton united

8

new town

9

fairview fc

10

valley athletic

11

oldcastle town

Overlap the ends by a finger width.

1. To make a long strip for the league table, fold a rectangle of thick paper in half, along its length. Cut along the fold, then glue the pieces together, like this.

This league table is shown in two parts so that it fits on the pages. The steps show you how to make one long one.

This long piece of paper will be the league table.

2. Press sticky tape along the join, to make it stronger. Then, fold the whole piece of paper in half along its length, with the tape on the inside.

Leave a gap between each cut and bigger spaces at the top and bottom.

If your league has more or fewer than 20 teams, just make the correct number of slots and shirts.

3. Make 20 cuts into the fold, cutting about halfway across the paper. Then, unfold the league table and lay it with the tape facing down.

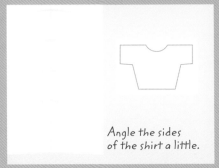

Angle the sides of the shirt a little.

4. Draw a shirt on a piece of thin cardboard. Make the bottom of the shirt narrow enough to slot easily into the league table. Then, cut it out.

Put the teams in their current order in the league.

5. Draw around the shirt 20 times on pieces of paper, then cut them out. Decorate them and add team names, then push them into the slots.

Write the numbers going down, so that '20' is at the bottom.

Move the shirts around as the teams change position in the league.

6. Write numbers 1-20 above the shirts. Write the name of your league on a piece of paper, then cut it out and glue it at the bottom of the table.

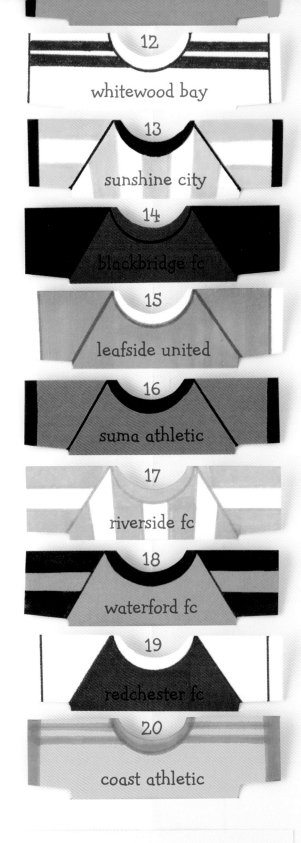

12 — whitewood bay

13 — sunshine city

14 — blackbridge fc

15 — leafside united

16 — suma athletic

17 — riverside fc

18 — waterford fc

19 — redchester fc

20 — coast athletic

CHAMPION FOOTBALL LEAGUE

Muddy park picture

1. Mix some green paint and water in a plastic pot, to make watery paint. Brush the paint all over a piece of thin white cardboard, then let it dry.

2. Using a pencil, draw a player's head, then draw his shirt and shorts. Draw his arms and legs, then add boots, socks and a football.

3. Pressing quite hard with coloured pencils, fill in the shirt and shorts. Fill in his face, hair, arms and legs, then fill in the football, too.

You could draw bags or sweaters for goal posts, and a keeper sliding through the mud to stop the ball.

To draw a picture of friends playing football in a park, use a big piece of cardboard, and draw lots of players in step 2.

4. To make 'mud', pour thick brown paint into a pot and mix in lots of white glue. Then, brush patches of mud around the player.

5. Dip a finger into the paint, then fingerprint footprints leading away from the player's boots. Print muddy patches on the player, too.

Penalty shoot-out game

Make the strip the width of the two rectangles.

1. Cut two rectangles of thin cardboard that are the same size, one white and one green. Then, cut a long strip of thick cardboard, about 3cm wide.

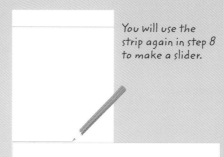

You will use the strip again in step 8 to make a slider.

2. Fold the white rectangle in half, then unfold it again. Lay the cardboard strip along the top and draw along it, then draw a line at the bottom, too.

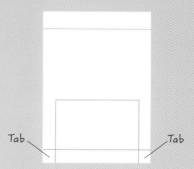

Tab   Tab

3. Draw a goal in the bottom half of the cardboard, across the line, like this. The little squares below the line will be tabs for the goal's base.

Play this game with a friend. Take it in turns to be the goalkeeper or the penalty-taker.

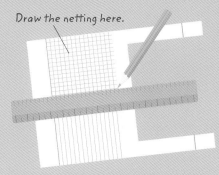

Draw the netting here.

4. Cut out the goal. Then, use a ruler and a blue pencil to draw lots of lines for netting. Draw them between the top line from step 2 and the middle fold.

Fold the tabs before you glue them onto the base.

5. To make the goal, fold the cardboard along the top line from step 2 to make a base. Then, fold the goal in half and glue the tabs onto the base.

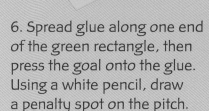

6. Spread glue along one end of the green rectangle, then press the goal onto the glue. Using a white pencil, draw a penalty spot on the pitch.

7. To make a stand for the goalkeeper, cut a strip of thick paper that is a little taller than the goal. Fold it in half, then fold up the bottom to make flaps.

Glue the stand in the middle of the slider.

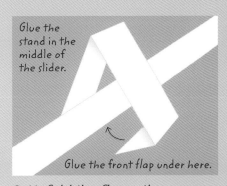

Glue the front flap under here.

8. Unfold the flaps, then open the paper a little. Glue the back flap to the bottom of the slider from step 2. Then, fold the front back and glue its flap on, too.

9. Draw a goalkeeper on a separate piece of paper. Fill him in with felt-tip pens and cut around him. Then, glue the goalkeeper onto the stand.

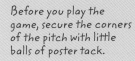

Before you play the game, secure the corners of the pitch with little balls of poster tack.

10. Fold up the ends of the slider. Slide it between the goal posts and the netting. Make a ball from a piece of foil and place it on the penalty spot.

How to play (2 players)

One player tries to score a penalty by flicking the ball at the goal. The other player tries to block the shot by moving the goalkeeper from side to side with the slider.

Move the slider with your thumbs.

Bouncing ball card

Fold

1. For the card, fold a square of thin cardboard in half, then unfold it again. Fold the front of the card over, so that its edge lines up with the fold.

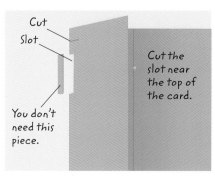

Cut
Slot

You don't need this piece.

Cut the slot near the top of the card.

2. Make a cut near the top of the second fold. Make a slot below it for the ball, by snipping two tiny cuts and cutting from one to the other. Unfold the card.

Glue the footballer a little way below the slot.

3. Draw a footballer and a ball on thick paper. Make the player small enough to fit below the slot. Cut them out, then glue the footballer onto the card.

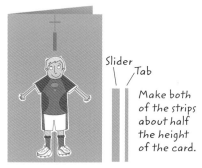

Slider   Tab

Make both of the strips about half the height of the card.

4. For the slider that makes the ball move, cut a cardboard strip that fits through the cut at the top of the fold. Then, cut a narrower strip for a tab.

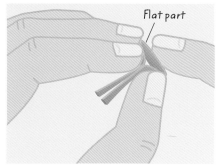

Flat part

5. Bend the tab into a loop. Then, hold it a little way below the looped end and push down on the loop to flatten it. Glue the ball onto the flat part.

Try making a goalkeeper throwing and catching a ball.

You could make a card with a footballer playing "keepy-uppy" with a ball.

To make a card with two players passing a ball, turn the card sideways, and make a slot near the bottom.

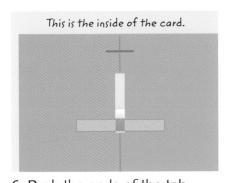

This is the inside of the card.

6. Push the ends of the tab through the slot in the card, then open the card. Push the tab to the bottom of the slot, and fold back the ends.

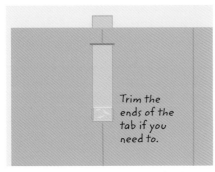

Trim the ends of the tab if you need to.

7. Push the slider through the cut in the card until its end is over the tab. Fold the ends of the tab over the slider, then tape them down.

Hold the slider here.

8. Close the card and push the slider so that the ball touches the footballer's head. Hold the slider, then move it up and down to make the ball 'bounce'.

Stand-up cheering fan

Make the top of the shirt touch the fold.

1. Fold a rectangle of thick paper in half, with its short ends together. Then, with the fold at the top, draw a football fan's shirt, like this.

You could give a happy fan as a card, and write a message inside.

Don't cut the sleeves off the back layer.

2. Keeping the paper folded, cut out the shirt through both layers. Cut the sleeves off the front layer of the shirt. Then, turn the shirt over.

The head and arms need to overlap the outline of the shirt.

3. Lay the top half of the shirt on thick paper and draw around it, then lift it off. Draw a head and a curved shape for the arms, then cut them out.

Make the arms come out of the sleeves.

4. Spread glue on the middle part of the arms and press them inside the shirt. Then, turn the head over and glue it onto the shirt.

26

For a striped scarf, cut and glue on lots of short strips of paper, then trim off their ends.

RIVER CITY FC

Open out the bottom of the shirt a little to make the fan stand up.

Instead of cutting out a fan's hat in steps 5 and 6, you could cut out a shape for hair instead.

Draw the scarf overlapping the hands.

5. Lay the fan on thick paper. Draw around the top of the head and arms, then lift off the fan. Using the outlines as a guide, draw a hat and scarf.

6. Cut out the shapes and erase any pencil lines. Then, cut a paper bobble to go on the hat. Make lots of tiny cuts around its edge, then glue it on.

7. Make tiny cuts in the ends of the scarf, then glue the hat and scarf onto the fan. Glue on a paper shield as a logo, then draw his hair and face.

Springy footballer

Press lightly with a pencil.

1. Draw a rounded shape for a footballer's head near the top of a piece of thick white paper. Draw his hair, then add his ears and face.

2. Draw a neck below the head, then draw the footballer's shirt. Draw shorts, then add a football overlapping the shirt a little, like this.

3. Draw an arm curving around the ball. Then, draw the other arm. Draw a logo and stripes on the shirt, then add a pattern on the ball.

You can't see the 'springs' on the footballers in this photo, because they are hidden behind them.

Look at this picture for ideas of how to draw other footballers.

4. Draw the footballer's legs, then add socks and boots. Draw studs and laces on the boots, then draw over all of the lines with a black pencil.

5. Fill in the footballer with pencils. Cut him out, leaving a border. For the 'spring', cut a strip of thick paper, half as tall as the footballer.

6. Glue one end of the spring to the back of the footballer's head. Bend the other end back and gently press it onto a window using poster tack.

This footballer is practising his ball skills.

Try making a goalkeeper wearing a long-sleeved top and gloves.

Winning fans coach picture

Print the driver's hands with your little finger.

1. Draw a big coach on paper, then cut it out and glue it onto a large piece of paper. Draw wheels by drawing around and around with a black pencil.

2. Cut two round hubcaps from white paper and glue them onto the wheels. Cut three windows and a panel for the side of the coach, then glue them on, too.

3. For the fans' faces, mix some thick paints on an old plate. Fingerprint lots of faces on the windows. Then, add ears and necks with a thin brush.

Red City Football Club

Draw scarves on some of the fans.

4. Leave the paint to dry completely, then use a thin black pen to draw the fans' shoulders and arms. Fill them all in with a bright pencil.

Red City Footb

Draw some flags and streamers, too.

5. Draw hats and hair on the fans, then fill them in with pencils. Then, use the black pen to draw happy faces and extra lines on the hair.

Red

6. Add lights and other details such as a steering wheel and wheel arches on the coach. Write the team name on the panel on the side of the coach.

31

Trophy cup pen pot

The rectangles are for a cup that will slide over the jar.

1. For the cup, cut two paper rectangles that wrap around a jar. Bend each one around until the edges meet, then pinch the paper to mark its middle.

Spread glue right up to the folds.

2. Fold the sides of each rectangle into the middle. Unfold them again, then turn one rectangle over and spread glue all over its side flaps.

You could tie ribbons onto the handles of your cup.

Fill the jar inside the cup with pens, pencils and other bits and bobs.

Add decorations with a silver pen if you have one.

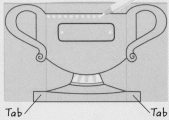

Tab   Tab

3. Press the other rectangle on top, lining up the folds. Draw a cup on the middle section, then add handles and tabs on the side flaps.

4. To make the handles, pinch the paper in the middle of each 'hole' and make a cut. Carefully push a scissor blade into the cut, then cut around both holes.

5. Cut around the cup and tabs, then fold back the tabs. Glue the tabs to the back of the cup, then slide the cup over the jar, with the handles sticking out.

Photographic manipulation by Nick Wakeford and Will Dawes
First published in 2014 by Usborne Publishing Ltd., 83-85 Saffron Hill, London, EC1N 8RT, England www.usborne.com